T0020927

BEYOND BULGER ROCK

BEYOND BULGER ROCK

JAY KLONOWSKI

TATE PUBLISHING
AND ENTERPRISES, LLC

Published by Tate Publishing & Enterprises, LLC
127 E. Trade Center Terrace | Mustang, Oklahoma 73064 USA
1.888.361.9473 | www.tatepublishing.com

Tate Publishing is committed to excellence in the publishing industry. The company reflects the philosophy established by the founders, based on Psalm 68:11,
"The Lord gave the word and great was the company of those who published it."

Book design copyright © 2014 by Tate Publishing, LLC. All rights reserved.
Cover design by Jim Villaflores
Interior design by Jomar Ouano

Published in the United States of America

ISBN: 978-1-63122-777-6
Fiction / Biographical
14.09.09

n 1979, I was a twelve-year-old boy, and my sister, Emily, was fourteen. Looking back now, I had to believe that my father must have realized that my sister and I knew how to get off the Utah mountain and back home. My dad had to have figured it out not too long after he got caught in that old rusty bear trap.

The farthest back I could remember was kindergarten, because everyone called me dumb. I guessed it was because I didn't talk. Mom and Dad worked different shifts—Dad mostly worked days at the factory and Mom held a job at her friend's furniture shop on Dad's days off. I always stayed home with whichever one was off that day. The only time I really wanted to go anywhere was when Dad and I would make a trip to the hardware store to get supplies for things we were working on around the house. I always had fun finding these things in the store and going home and watching my dad build or fix things. It seemed he had great ideas and knew how to do anything, as every little boy thinks of his father.

My dad had to have everything just right. Some projects were small, others took days. When we started doing big projects, at first it would seem like we would never get done, but by the second day, I could tell all this work was turning into something great. And when we finished, my dad and I would step back and admire our work. It was so cool. Mom didn't think much of this. She would come home from work and either not say much or tell us that it was not what she wanted and how it could have been better if we had done it in a different way.

As the years went on, my dad didn't put as much effort into our projects anymore. I didn't know why; we had so much fun doing it.

Emily was in fourth grade now, so I must have been about seven years old. She was getting all Bs in school, which I thought was great. On the way home from school, she was so pumped to show off her report card. She ran into the house to show it to our mother.

"Mom, Mom! We got our report cards today, and I got all Bs!" she said.

As I walked into the house, my mom's only comment was to shut the door because when Emily ran inside yelling, she left it open. So in a soft voice, Emily again said, "Mom, I got all Bs."

My mom told her to stop saying *got*. "*Got* isn't a word!" She snapped. Emily put her report card on the counter and, with her head low, sulked off to the room my dad had built for her in the basement.

I went to my room, not knowing what to do. It seemed that even when I thought something was good, it was not. That's when I saw the trophy my dad gave me for winning at a miniature golf competition. I thought if I gave that to Emily, it would show her that I was proud of her for getting good grades. Since I don't talk, it was the only way I thought I could tell her. I took my trophy to the basement and when I was at Emily's door, I could hear her crying, so I just left and went back to my room.

My dad came home, and I ran to the door as Emily and I always did; only today Emily stayed in her room. My dad saw Emily's report card on the counter and saw she had all Bs.

"Wow that's great," he said.

My mom said, "Don't make such a fuss over her, she can be doing better."

I didn't know whether my dad ever told Emily that he was happy about her grades or not. I liked to think he did.

When I turned nine and Emily was eleven, she didn't put too much effort into her grades anymore. She was mostly interested in running around with some new friends. I was too young to get the whole story, but I heard Emily and her friends were in someone's house and that the parents weren't home and she stole some things. I didn't know what was going on with her, but I thought it had to do with Dad working all the time now and not being around as much as he used to be. He was taking as much overtime at the factory as he could get. I guessed we needed the money.

Now that Dad was working so much, I would go to work with my mom. She told me, "Jacob, you can help me at work with vacuuming and stuff." I thought that sounded like fun, I always had such a blast working with Dad.

It was the first time I was going to the shop, so I didn't know the other ladies. They all seemed really nice, coming up to me with smiles on their faces and saying, "Hi, cutie, how are you? Are you going to help us today?"

My mom would then tell the ladies who were shaking my hand and rubbing my head, "He is dumb, he doesn't talk."

All the ladies came up to me, smiling, and said, "Jacob, come with us, we can clean up over in this area first."

We went and started moving furniture and vacuuming. We sure were working hard and getting a lot done. The ladies would smile and thank me for stuff all the time. We sat down for lunch, and they would tell me funny stories; we had a great time. At the end of the day when we were about to go home, my mom asked if I did anything, and I thought she could already tell just by looking at the difference in the room. Then one of the ladies said, "Yes, he worked real hard, and we had a lot of fun."

"You must not have worked too hard if you had fun. You will need to do a better job next time," my mom said.

I was twelve now and lost interest in going to work with my mom. Emily and I were thinking we were old enough to stay home by ourselves. We thought Dad might feel the same, but if he said yes, Mom would say no. That was just the way she was, so we knew we couldn't ask Dad first. When it was time for Mom to go to work, Emily said it was fine if I would stay home with her and she would watch me. She had thought that my mom would be proud of her not getting into trouble now for a long time and taking on some responsibility.

Instead, Mom said, "What are you going to do, just sit around here and do nothing or go out and get into trouble?"

"No." Emily protested. "I will stay home with Jacob and get some of the housework done so there isn't so much to do when you and Dad get home."

"Don't bother. You don't do anything right anyways, and then I have to do it over again. Jacob can stay home with you. He doesn't do anything at the shop anyways." And then she left for work.

I just stayed in my room all day, and Emily did some housework and then went down to her room to read one of her books. I thought reading took her mind off things that were bothering her in some way.

One day, Emily was telling me a story she'd read about a twenty-foot-tall arched rock up in the mountains near our house. Not a lot of people had seen it because it was such a long hike, and there were no roads up there.

She thought it was so cool and she talked about it all day until my dad got home from work. She told him all about it, and I was hearing the story all over again.

Emily was finally excited about something again, which was really cool because I hadn't seen her excited about anything in a long time. She asked my dad if we could hike up there one day. My dad said he had heard about this arched rock in the mountains before.

The door opened, and now my mom was home from work. Emily stopped talking about it and she looked like she had just been defeated before she even got started. My dad told Emily that the arched rock was about forty-eight miles up into the mountains. Mom asked if we were talking about that stupid rock up there, before anyone could say anything she went on to say, "No, it's not about forty-eight miles, it's about fifty." Emily just left and went down to her room. My dad could tell Emily was finally excited about something again and he didn't want this to go away. My dad, who never really talked too much because it seemed whatever he said around Mom was wrong anyway, stood up and told her, "We are going to hike up there!"

My mom said, "I'm not hiking up there to see some stupid rock that's probably not even real."

"That sounds good to me," Dad said. For the first time, my mom didn't know what to say. She didn't say anything. *Anything*. Dad went down to Emily's room. "Make a list of supplies we will need, it's a two-day hike just to get up there." That's all he needed to say, and Emily knew we were going to hike to the arched rock on the mountain.

She started right away and worked into the night. I didn't think she even slept at all; she was so excited. The next day, Dad came home from work, and we went right down to Emily's room and started planning.

My dad said, "The first day, we will hike to Bulger Rock." Bulger Rock could be seen from our house way up on the mountain. I guessed they called it Bulger Rock because it was one big rock bulging out the side of the mountain.

He added, "That's about halfway, and we will camp there the first night. The second day, we will hike the rest of the way to find the arched rock and then we will set up and camp there for two days and search together until we find it. I've never seen a real photo of the arched rock, only drawings. After we find it, we will pack up and head back to Bulger Rock, camp for the night, and then hike down to the house the next morning. So we will need six days of supplies for three people. We will go to the army surplus store tomorrow when I get home from work."

"What if you have to work overtime?" Emily asked. He said he wouldn't need to work overtime anymore. Sure enough, the next day, Dad was home at the time he used to be years ago.

We went straight to the army surplus and bought a brand-new tent, three sleeping bags, tarp, compass, three canteens, backpacks, binoculars, fishing pole, fold-up grill, and he bought me a really cool survival tool with a saw, a knife, and a pair of pliers, scissors, and tweezers; it even fit right on my belt. It was cool, and so I started wearing it right away.

The next day, Dad got home from work, and we went to Emily's room again. He said, "Now, we will need a list of food. We will go to the grocery store when I get home from work tomorrow. We will be leaving for Bulger Rock the next morning. I'm on vacation next week, so we have seven days."

The next day, Dad got home from work, and Emily had her list ready for the grocery store. It seemed to be a lot of food, but I thought that was better than not having enough. When we got home, we started packing our backpacks.

"Everyone will carry their own sleeping bag, and I will carry the tent. The rest, we will divide up equally between us, leaving room to pack the food in the morning," Dad said.

The next morning, we were up at dawn. We packed the rest of our supplies and told Mom, "We are heading up the mountain and we would be back in six days after we find the arched rock."

"Yes, well, don't get all excited about something that's probably not even there. You are setting yourself up for disappointment," Mom said. We just left and started out for Bulger Rock.

About noon, Dad said it was time to take a break. We all sat down when Emily pulled out a bag of wild berries. My dad asked her where she got them.

"I picked them last night before dark in the woods behind the house," she said.

We all sat for about a half hour and enjoyed Emily's wild berries. Then we threw on our packs, and that was when Dad said, "Emily, you will lead from here, since this is your quest."

Emily looked a little nervous, but she said, "Yes, you're right, this is my quest." So we set out, knowing Emily would get us there. You can see Bulger Rock from anywhere on this side of the mountain.

It was almost dark when Dad said, "All right, we're here. Let's set up camp and get a fire going so we can cook some dinner."

Emily and I started gathering firewood, while Dad set up the tent. We built a fire, and Dad pulled out some hotdogs and hamburgers that he packed frozen this morning and were now thawed out after hiking all day.

I thought that was brilliant. We all ate too much, and Dad said we would need it; we were only halfway, after all. After dinner, we went into the tent and slept really good, being tired from hiking all day.

We woke up the next morning at first sunlight. Dad boiled hot water over the fire for his coffee, and Emily and I had some granola bars and a juice box. We took down the tent, got our packs together, and set out to find the arched rock. My legs were very stiff from hiking up the mountain the day before, but as we went on, they started to stretch out and feel better. We were getting very tired today, so we took more breaks. That was when Dad told us, "I've never been up this far, I've never been beyond Bulger Rock. So from here on out, it's all new to all of us."

We started out again until we were almost to the top of the mountain; then we looked down on Bulger Rock.

"Where from here to the arched rock?" My dad asked Emily.

"It's in the valley," Emily replied.

That was when we looked and saw that the mountain was one huge circle and the center was one big valley. That was the first time I thought this arched rock might be real. The mountain from the sky must look like one big doughnut. The arched rock was down in this valley, so we set out down to the other side of the mountain and into the valley. As we did, we could see less and less of Bulger Rock, the only landmark we knew. It wasn't much longer before we couldn't see Bulger Rock at all. Now, we were at the bottom of the valley and we didn't see any arched rock.

Dad said, "Okay, let's set up camp and we'll search in the morning."

He started dicing up some potatoes he had packed, put them in some aluminum foil, and threw the whole thing right on the fire. Later, he pulled them out using two sticks, unwrapped them, put salt and pepper on them, shook them, and then threw them back in the fire. A while later, he pulled them out, and then we ate all of them. Man, they were good. Dad stoked the fire and made it really big and bright. He then got out his compass and said, "We came in from the south, so let's search up the north side of the valley in the morning." Emily thought that was a great plan.

In the morning, my dad handed Emily the compass and said, "Take us up to the north side of the valley."
Emily led the way. We searched all day, but we didn't see any arched rock. That night at the campfire, my dad said, "Tomorrow we will search the east side of the valley."

Emily and I agreed. The next morning, Emily took us up to the east side of the valley and still, after searching all day, the arched rock was nowhere to be seen. That night back at camp, Emily and I already knew the plan for the next day, because there was only one place left to search—the west side of the valley. That must be where the arched rock is, I thought.

We didn't sleep well that night. I thought we were going back and forth in our minds: Will we find it? Or is it not real and just a story?

In the morning, Dad told us, "We only have one day's worth of food left, so try to make do with less today. If the arched rock isn't on the west side of this valley, we have to head home tomorrow no matter what."

We set out for our final search. We were hiking for about two hours when we came up to a lake and realized that to search the west side of this valley, we would have to walk around this entire lake. We did not stop, knowing this was our last chance to find the arched rock. Emily also noticed that the same kind of wild berries that she brought from our house grew around the lake, so she picked some to take back to camp. I thought that was a great idea, since we were almost out of food.

"Maybe we can catch some fish and cook them on the fire tonight and save the rest of our food for the hike back home," Dad said.

Just then, we heard a loud snap and my dad started to scream. I never heard my dad scream like that before. Emily and I ran to him. There was a metal thing wrapped around his leg, and he fell to the ground in pain. I grabbed the two jaws and pulled as hard as I could, but it wouldn't budge.

My dad said, "Push down on each of the sides of the jaws and then pull them apart."

Emily stepped on the sides, one foot on each, and I pulled as hard as I could. It hardly moved, but it was enough for my dad to get his leg out. He sat there holding his leg as blood ran down to the ground. Emily grabbed my survival tool off my belt. Dad took his shirt off, and Emily took the shirt, cut it into two pieces, wrapped one half around his leg, and tied the other half tight to his leg. It was like they knew what the other was thinking without saying a word.

"Just let me sit here a while until I catch my breath," my dad said.

I took my survival tool back from Emily and started looking for a tree branch. It took me a while to find just the right one, and I thought it would work great. I sawed the branch off the tree and then cut the branch above the V, cutting them off evenly. It made a makeshift crutch. I went back to my dad and Emily. She was helping Dad up off the ground. I handed him the crutch, and he said, "This will work perfectly. We must head straight back to camp so we can make it by dark. I won't be able to go very fast, so it will take some time."

He put his one arm around me and the other over his crutch, and then we headed straight back to camp. Dad was right; it was starting to get dark when we got back. Emily and I brought Dad straight into the tent, took one sleeping bag, and put it under his leg to keep it raised. The bleeding had seemed to stop, so Emily took the torn shirt off my dad's leg. She cleaned them with some water from her canteen and set them out to dry.

"What was that thing that snapped around your leg?" Emily asked Dad.

"It was an old rusty bear trap, and I'm lucky because if it hadn't been so rusty, that thing would have taken my leg right off." Emily took some more water to clean my dad's leg, but he told her, "No, don't use all the water. You and Jacob will need it to hike out first thing in the morning and get some help back to me."

"Don't worry, I filled all three canteens with fresh water and picked all these berries on the way back from the lake," Emily said. She pulled out a bagful of berries and also filled every pocket she had. We had enough berries for two days.

"Wow, that was good thinking," my dad said.

I could tell by the look on Emily's face that she felt very proud when she said, "I'm not leaving you, Dad, so, Jacob, you'll have to hike out alone to get help."

I nodded and started to fill my pack, preparing to leave at first light. Emily put another full canteen of water next to my pack, while Dad grabbed a handful of beef jerky we'd brought along.

"Take this with you, Jacob. We will be fine. Emily can go back down to the lake and catch us some fish," Dad said.

"Yes," Emily chimed in, "I can go get fish and more water tomorrow." Then she asked my dad if he had the compass.

"No, I must have lost it when I fell down by the lake."

"I'll look for it tomorrow when I go fishing." Emily and I were trying to start a fire when she went on to say, "Which way did we come in? We've been all over this valley, and I'm all turned around. If the lake is in the west side of the valley and Dad said we came in from the south, now which way is south? We don't have the compass"—then she pointed—"it must be that way." I looked at the direction she was pointing to and thought that was the way I would go in the morning.

We were just getting back into the tent to get a good night's rest when my dad said, "Jacob, I didn't know you were so strong to just rip that bear trap off my leg like that and help me all the way back here to camp."

For the first time in my life, I felt something come over me. I lifted my head and looked into my father's eyes. I was proud and I knew he was proud of me too. I slept very well that night, and at first light, I was ready to go. I set out in the direction Emily and I agreed must be south back to Bulger Rock, the only landmark we knew.

I hiked all day and finally made it to the top of the mountain, but looking down the other side, I didn't see any rock. Now, do I walk the entire top of the rim until I find it? And which way do I go? What if I go the wrong way? Will I be getting farther away? I just stood there, not knowing what to do, and I was about to lose sunlight, so I would have to camp here.

I didn't sleep very well that night, thinking all night about what I should do. I decided to head back down into the valley and let Emily and Dad know. I would try the other way tomorrow morning. Emily and I must have guessed wrong about which way was south.

I woke up very early the next morning and started hiking back to camp before the sun was even up. I had to tell them I didn't know the way out. I made it back to camp in what seemed like no time at all, and when I got there, I saw Emily cleaning some fish and Dad sitting up and cutting up the last of the potatoes. It was good to see him sitting up and doing something.

He stood up when he saw me, and Emily turned around and said, "You didn't find it?" in a very chipper voice. "Oh, well, you can try again tomorrow." She didn't seem to be very worried about anything. My dad walked toward me on his crutch and put his hand on my shoulder and said, "It's not your fault, Jacob. I didn't plan for anything like this."

"I will throw the potatoes on now and start the fish here in a little bit," Emily said. When I saw she had three fish cleaned and seasoned, it was like she knew I was going to be here. I couldn't get over Emily; she sounded different, and even looked different. It was almost like she was happy we were here. Maybe that was it—she was happy, even with everything we were going through.

I was also very happy. It seemed we agreed on stuff, we knew what the other needed, and no one was arguing. Dad even seemed more relaxed, even after almost getting his leg cut off. We all sat around the campfire enjoying the great dinner Emily made for us, and she talked more than I had ever heard her talk before, telling us stories about stuff she never told us before. Dad and I just listened to her talk well into the night. We all slept very soundly that night.

In the morning, we sat and listened to Emily talk even more, and we ate a bunch of her berries. For whatever reason, none of us were in a hurry for me to get going to find the way back home. Dad was walking a little better now, but not well enough for a two-day hike. I figured I should start packing for my hike out. Emily gave me another full canteen of water and caught me off guard when she grabbed me and gave me a hug. Then she stepped back with her hands on my shoulders, looked me in the eyes, and said, "I love you."

I threw my pack over my shoulder and said, "I love you too."

My dad looked shocked, and Emily started to cry. None of us said anything else, and I walked away.

The whole day, I kept thinking, should I have stayed and explained to them that I always knew I could talk and why I didn't? Or would I have said something wrong? Or was it just better left this way? I was thinking these thoughts when suddenly I saw a big rock. But I was not on the top of the mountain yet, so I thought it couldn't be Bulger Rock.

I kept heading toward it though; that was the only rock I'd seen since we'd been in the valley. When I got a little closer, I realized I was looking at the arched rock. It was shaped like a rainbow made of different colored rocks—red, gray, white, and brown—and it was bigger than I had imagined. It was all of twenty feet tall and twenty feet wide. I stood underneath it and when I looked up at the bottom, I kind of lost my balance and became disoriented and overwhelmed. I thought of going to tell my dad and Emily that the arched rock is here, but I couldn't. I had to find our way back home, and finding the arched rock was Emily's quest. Should I somehow let her find the arched rock, letting her think I didn't know where it was? Yes, I would find our way out and somehow get her in this area and let her find it.

I continued up the mountain, and when I got to the top, right in front of me was Bulger Rock. That was when I realized the arched rock was just in the back of Bulger Rock. We didn't see the arched rock on the way in because from this direction, all you could see are trees that were growing over it. But coming from this other direction, you could see it really good. I walked closer to Bulger Rock so I could look down to the town and set up camp for the night. When I could see the town, I stopped and just looked at it. My head went down, and I lost all of the great feelings I had been feeling for this last week. I realized I might not want to go back home, but enough of that. I needed to get my dad and Emily out of the valley and home safely.

I didn't sleep very much that night. I kept tossing back and forth, thinking, do I want to go home, or do I want to stay in the valley? I woke up the next morning knowing no matter what I wanted, I needed to get help. I was starting to pack for the hike down to town when the morning sun hit something shiny by the rock. I went over and picked it up. It was the compass! Emily had already been here, she knew how to get home, she must have hiked up here the day I hiked up the wrong side of the valley.

This changed things. Emily didn't want to leave the valley either, but that was not right; Dad needed help. Before I even knew what I was doing, I was hiking back to the valley. I needed to get to Emily. I felt like I couldn't get to her fast enough. I was almost running back to camp. When I got down to the bottom of the valley, I could see my dad walking around in the woods gathering firewood, which was good; his leg must have been feeling much better. Plus, I needed to talk to Emily before he knew I was back.

I started walking really slow so I wouldn't make too much noise. When I got closer to camp, Emily was by the fish-cleaning board, and when she saw me, she said, "You didn't find the way out?"

As I set the compass on the cleaning board, she looked at me like I had just kicked her really hard. "We need to get Dad out of here and then we can decide what we want to do, but we need to get him help first," I told her.

"Yes, you're right. I don't know what I was thinking."

"I know what you were thinking because I was thinking the same thing." That was when Dad heard us. He turned around and started walking toward us.

"Hey, did you find your way out?" he said.

I turned and looked at Emily and said, "Yes, I found the way out."

"Good, my leg feels much better, but I don't want to overdo it, so we can head out at first light. Tonight, we can cook up the last of Emily's fish and save the last of the beef jerky and granola bars for the hike out."

Emily said, "I have more berries and I filled up the canteens with fresh water, so we should be good to go."

That night, we sat around the campfire and talked until it was dark. Neither my dad nor Emily asked me why I never talked until now; they just let me talk on and on. They never stopped me or corrected me, they just let me talk. It felt great.

We all slept really well that night, and in the morning, we ate the rest of the granola bars and took down the tent. While Dad was having his coffee, Emily and I packed up the rest of our supplies. I took the tent on my pack to make things lighter on my dad. Dad grabbed his crutch, which he had cut shorter now so it was more like a cane. We put our packs on, and I told Emily to lead us out of the valley. She took us straight to the arched rock.

"Wow, you found it!" my dad said.

"Yes, yes, I did," Emily replied. She didn't seem overly excited, and that was when I realized that she had been here before. She didn't need to tell us, didn't need to say "I told you so." It just seemed it was enough that she knew it was real.

My dad went on and on saying, "I can't believe it! You found it! The arched rock...it is really here! That makes it all worth it, everything we've been through together in the valley. I love you, kids, so much."

"We love you too, Dad," Emily and I said at the same time.

We just stood there and looked at the rock for a while. It looked more beautiful this time. I didn't know if it was because the sun was shining on it, or if it was because I was with Emily and my dad.

A while later, we left and then headed up the rest of the way to Bulger Rock. We all felt great, even Dad, who wasn't even using his makeshift cane. When we reached the top of the mountain, we could see a couple of men. My dad started calling out to them by name.

"Hey, Mike, Dave, what are you doing up here?"

One of the men turned and said, "You didn't show up for work after your vacation. We asked your wife what happened, and she told us you and the kids came up here, so we figured we better come up and find out if you guys are all right."

"Yes," my dad said, looking at Emily and me. "We are great, no need to worry, we are great." We walked over to the campfire the men had going, since it was about to get dark, and then we all started talking. Neither of the men asked us what we were doing up here; they just went on and on telling Emily and me stories about how great our dad was—that Dad could fix anything and build anything, that he was a great man, and that when any family in town needed help with something, he was the first one there to take care of anything they needed. It was really cool meeting these two men from town and listening to them say such good things about my dad. We'd never heard anything good about our dad before; all we ever heard was what he did wrong.

Emily and I set up the tent and slipped into our sleeping bags. As the light from the campfire shone through the tent, we listened to the two men tell stories about how my dad was one of most respected men in town. And then we fell asleep.

We got up early the next morning and got ready for the hike home. The men were loud as they picked on each other, laughing all the way down the mountain and telling silly stories about each other, and even telling funny stories about themselves. When Dave said to Mike, "What, are you dumb?" they started laughing again and went on to tell another silly story. That was when I realized that my dad never said to anyone that I was dumb.

We were almost to the house when Emily looked back up at Bulger Rock, so I stopped, and we looked at each other and then back at Bulger Rock. She then asked me, "What are we doing?"

I told her, "I don't know."

We continued down the mountain toward the house. It seemed that Emily and I felt we were leaving home instead of heading home. As we walked into our front yard, my dad and the two men were still laughing and telling stories. When my mom walked out of the house, all went quiet.

"We found them, they are fine," Mike said to her.

"I'm glad you guys are all right," Dave told us as he threw his backpack in his truck. After some good-byes, he left, with Mike right behind him.

Emily and I were walking into the house when my mom asked, "Did you find your stupid rock?" Emily and I just put our heads down…My dad stepped in and said,

"Yes, we did find it, and it was beautiful. I'm so glad we went."

"Well, I hope so. You were gone long enough, make sure you put all your crap away. I don't want it lying around the house all week," my mom said.

Emily and my dad started to unpack their supplies, and I went behind. When Emily was done, she went straight to her room. My dad saw me pick up one of their water canteens and put it on my pack, but not taking anything else out of my pack. I took my pack and went to my room.

About fifteen minutes later, my bedroom door opened, and my dad reached down toward my pack. I wasn't sure what he was going to do when he set the compass on top of my pack. He turned to me, and I thought he was going to ask me what I was planning to do, but he just said, "I love you, son. Good night."

I should have known after all we had been through together that he already knew what I had planned to do. So I just said, "I love you too, Dad. Good night."

CPSIA information can be obtained at www.ICGtesting.com
Printed in the USA
LVOW10*0004041016

507289LV00007B/22/P